SASHI
Adopts a Brother

Linda Greiner

Illustrator
Morgan Spicer

BROWN BOOKS KIDS

Sashi Adopts a Brother

Brown Books Kids
16250 Knoll Trail Drive, Suite 205
Dallas, Texas 75248
www.BrownBooksKids.com
(972) 381-0009

A New Era in Publishing™

ISBN 978-1-61254-856-2
LCCN 2015942007

Printed in the United States
10 9 8 7 6 5 4 3 2 1

For more information or to contact the author, please go to www.NJSheltieMom.com

32014 1581

Dedication

This book is dedicated to my Sashi, a truly remarkable little dog, to all Shelties looking for their very own forever homes, and to the volunteers in Sheltie Rescue working tirelessly to make these adoptions possible.

Acknowledgments

I would like to thank my family, friends, and coworkers for their continued support and encouragement. A big shout-out for the extremely talented Morgan Spicer and her illustrations bringing Sashi's stories to life, to the wonderful creative team at Brown Books Kids, and to Shetland Sheepdog Placement Services of New Jersey for approving my adoption application so I could bring my princess home.

Sashi was a Shetland Sheepdog—a Sheltie. She was a herding dog. Sashi's original family didn't want her because she chased cars, bikes, and running children. She was adopted by a new family. They understood that she was born to herd everyone and everything into neat little groups.

Sashi loved her new family very much. There were a mommy and a little girl named Anna. A few years after they adopted Sashi, her family decided to help other Shelties who needed new homes. They started to work for Shetland Sheepdog Rescue, an organization of volunteers who provide Shelties with temporary "foster" homes until they are adopted.

Sashi made sure the "foster dogs" knew she was the ruling princess of her home. She expected them to let her be first in everything—first to go outdoors, first to be fed, first to be petted and cuddled.

Foster
Sheltie Rescue

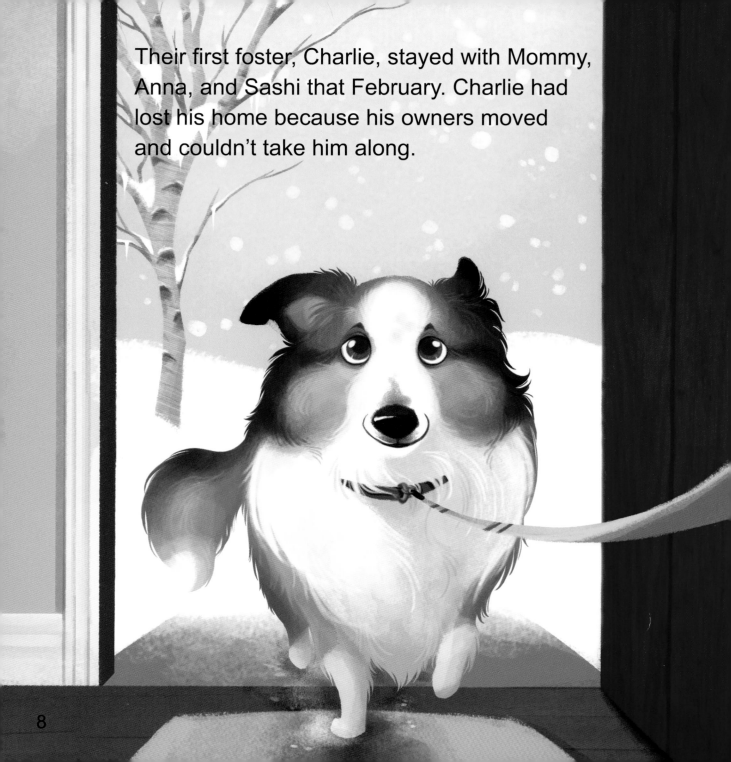

Their first foster, Charlie, stayed with Mommy, Anna, and Sashi that February. Charlie had lost his home because his owners moved and couldn't take him along.

8

Charlie taught Sashi how to climb snow drifts. Sashi liked that. When she was on top of a snow drift, she could survey her whole kingdom. That's what she thought a princess should do.

Charlie was adopted by a family who trained him to be a therapy dog. He visited people in hospitals to help them feel better, which helped them to get better faster.

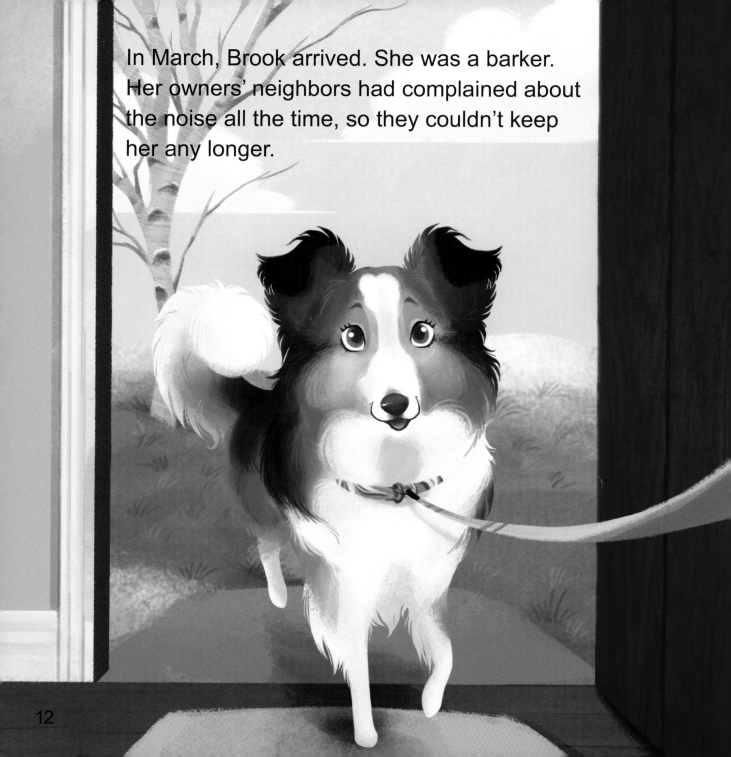

In March, Brook arrived. She was a barker. Her owners' neighbors had complained about the noise all the time, so they couldn't keep her any longer.

12

Sashi was very annoyed at having another girl in the house, and she growled at Brook all the time. Sashi didn't want Brook to think she could be a princess, too. She was very glad when Brook left for her new home.

The next foster was Sammie. His owner had allergies and sneezed every time Sammie was in the room. The doctor said Sammie would have to go.

Sammie liked to chase the laser light toy. Sashi thought he was a little strange. Princesses did not chase laser lights.

The people who adopted Sammie ran a store at the beach. They made him the store manager because he always escorted their customers to the register.

Then along came Buddy. He was only a year and a half old. He was big for a Sheltie—almost the size of a collie.

Buddy leaped out of his crate as if he'd been shot from a cannon. Then he jumped up on Mommy and Anna and knocked them to the floor.

Buddy chewed everything: furniture, books, shoes, even windowsills.

He stole food off the counter. He dug up the garden.

Needless to say, he had lost his first home because of his bad behaviors.

19

Buddy loved to pester Sashi. He would bow, spin, and bark at Sashi until she couldn't stand it any longer and chased him—just what Buddy wanted.

Round and round the dining room table they would run,

up the stairs and down the stairs, and around the garden until they collapsed, exhausted.

Sashi had never had this much fun with the other fosters. He made her forget about being a princess. She hoped he would stay a long time. Buddy hoped he would stay, too. He liked making Sashi play in spite of herself.

But Mommy and Anna hoped Buddy would be adopted quickly.
He was so rowdy they didn't know what to do with him.

One day visitors came to meet Buddy. He was very rude and climbed all over them. The visitors didn't like that. They didn't want to adopt him.

Sashi was happy when they left. She and Buddy chased each other around the dining room table.

A few weeks later, Mommy and Anna took Buddy to see a different family. They met at a local park. But when Buddy saw other dogs, he barked like crazy and pulled on his leash. This family didn't want to adopt him, either.

Mommy and Anna returned home with Buddy. Sashi and Buddy chased each other up and down the stairs.

The following month, Mommy and Anna took Buddy to meet a third family. They had a cat. Buddy had never seen a cat before. Buddy growled at the cat, and the cat growled at Buddy. Buddy couldn't stay with that family.

When Mommy, Anna, and Buddy returned home,
Sashi chased Buddy around the garden.

Mommy and Anna suspected that Buddy was misbehaving on purpose at his adoption interviews. The Shetland Sheepdog Rescue people thought so, too. Buddy wanted to stay. Sashi wanted Buddy to stay, as well.

By now, five months had passed since Buddy arrived. Mommy said, "Buddy, I think Sashi has already adopted you. I'm going to fill out the paperwork to make it official."

Buddy didn't know what "paperwork" or "official" meant. He did know that he didn't have to meet any more new families. Buddy had already decided that he was going to stay forever.

Buddy and Sashi chased each other around the house every day. Buddy showed Sashi how to do his play bow and Sheltie spin. He taught her games like tug and tussle.

Buddy had found a forever home. Sashi had adopted a brother.

Sashi was still the ruling princess, but now Buddy was the prince—

with Sashi's permission, of course.

For the Adult Reader

Although Sashi's story is about Shetland sheepdogs, it applies to all purebreds, as well as "Heinz 57" dogs, in need of new homes. There are rescues across the country for just about every type of dog, all easily found with simple web searches.

The Shetland Sheepdog

The Shetland sheepdog, also known as the Sheltie, originated north of Scotland in the Shetland Islands. Known for their sensitive personalities, Shelties love nothing more than to please their owners, and they do best in an environment where gentleness and positive training methods are used.

If you are considering a Sheltie, you could not ask for a more loyal, wonderful companion. Each dog has a distinct personality, but there are basic traits shared by many, if not all, Shelties. They can be quite verbal. They are sound sensitive and often sound reactive, barking at anything from strangers at your door to ringing phones. They can be reserved, so early socialization is needed to keep them from being shy. Shelties are extremely intelligent and very active. They do well in obedience, agility, flyball, herding, and scent detection training. They are bred to work and will often "find a job" if you do not keep them occupied. They are hardwired to chase anything that moves—cars, bikes, birds, or toddlers.

The American Shetland Sheepdog Association has a rescue program with chapters in most states across the country. All rescue dogs are checked by the vet, brought up to date on shots, spayed/neutered, and receive any other medical care appropriate for their situation. Most are fostered in temporary homes, so the dog's personality can be evaluated to ensure the best match in a forever home. Everyone who works in the Sheltie Rescue is a volunteer.

For more information, please visit:
www.ASSA.org/
www.ASSA.org/Rescue.html

About the Author

Linda Greiner fell in love with Shelties when doing research on what type of dog to get for her sixteenth birthday. Many years later, instead of purchasing another puppy, she decided to contact the Shetland Sheepdog Placement Services of New Jersey (SSPSNJ) and adopted Sashi in 2001.

Hoping to find a suitable brother or sister for "the princess," Linda started fostering for SSPSNJ in 2003. Each dog has had a tale to tell. She is currently working on her third book in the series about Sashi and the rescues they have known and loved. A portion of sales proceeds from *Sashi, the Scared Little Sheltie* and *Sashi Adopts a Brother* are being donated to Sheltie Rescue.

About the Illustrator

Morgan Spicer is a children's book illustrator and the founder of Bark Point Studio. She has also designed album covers, children's pajamas, and children's board games, and she has worked as a background and character designer for PBS Sprout's *Sing It, Laurie!* She currently freelances for an Animation Studio in downtown New York while also creating custom animal art for her many Bark Point Studio fans. Morgan has created over 1,000 portraits, with a percentage of many of her commissions going to local and international animal rescue groups.